A UNICORN

DANCED IN THE WOODS

BY

CHRISTINE DAY

A BEAUTIFUL STORY TO HEAL THE EARTH

ILLUSTRATED BY JOHN WAKEFIELD

First Edition

ETHERIC BOOKS

'I have read this wonderful little book. It is unique and inspirational. The illustrations are an absolute delight, exceptional.'

James Herbert OBE, bestselling author

'I was struck by the sense of a child's mind and the world we quickly fail to see in adult life.'

Barry Fantoni, artist and writer

If you should stumble across a unicorn dancing in the

woods at twilight you will have deep dreams……….

Contents

Dream Deeply……..

© John Wakefield 2017

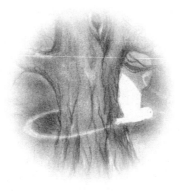

Circle of Oaks

A UNICORN wandered in the woods in autumn. Her body was white as snow quartz and her eyes cobalt blue glass tinged with sea green. The horn shimmered with starlight. The unicorn nibbled wild roses and drank the dew. She danced on her hind legs in the full Moon. To see her was to dream deeply. Her name was Maia.

1

The giant oak trees were dropping so many acorns and leaves that they formed a carpet into which the unicorn's hooves sank. The perfume of the dying leaves was divine. The Earth took them into her body like the Holy Communion. The trees talked to the unicorn. Their roots snaked down endlessly. They touched the crystalline energy and transmitted it up to the stars. They knew of the mysterious Crystal Skull, buried deeper than a hundred centuries. The oaks knew many mysteries and held their secrets with great pride.

Maia was alone but whole, connected. She talked to the stars. She played with butterflies in the honeyed warmth which brought forth plants and creatures and wishes and hopes that seemed to belong to spring. But all was destined to make the journey back to the womb of the Mother, to sleep out winter in a long, snug dream beneath the leaves and bracken. Going into death seemed so much

2

more alive. Frenzy before the stillness came and the soil was rock hard, pale with hoar frost. Sky clear blue as in an Italian altar painting.

Nobody knew the unicorn was in the woods. Children had glimpsed her, lost in fantasies as they skipped along. Blackberriers had disturbed deer and rabbits, awoken owls. A startled hare had skimmed across a field quicker than a heartbeat. But the unicorn kept her camouflage. She vibrated exceedingly fast and this was the secret of her invisibility. Only when she tired, because so many humans had been in the woods and stolen the energy, did she slow down and was in danger of being seen.

October days grew warmer, as if by mistake, and seemed longer when really shorter. The unicorn danced a dance of ecstasy.

Where had she come from this beast of light, so spiritual, sensitive and feminine? She was conceived in an act of imagination

3

powerful and holy, far beyond the comprehension of human minds. She had been as frail and perfect as a snowflake at first, tiny yet vast as a star – like the mighty oaks had once been acorns. The full Moon had watched over her birth. She always returned and kissed her. So the unicorn danced in the moonlight, her white body reflecting the beams.

She was older than legend and younger than a moment. She was born in the centre of a sweeping circle of ancient oaks, here four oaks stood in a line. The kingliest was Ariel where the white owl nested. There was also Dorc, Swinbourne, and Someil. All were majestic in their way and communed with eternity in the galaxies.

These giants nurtured the little unicorn.

The solitary owl, wise as a hermit, flew in and out of the

A UNICORN DANCED IN THE WOODS

branches of the four trees weaving intricate patterns in the ether. He was particularly watchful of the young creature. He was rarely seen, but in the shelter of darkness hooted a penetrating Om through apparent silence. Yet in the depth of night it was possible to hear the heart of the Earth beating, and the muffled expression of countless nocturnal creatures followed the evensong prayers of the birds as they flew against the delicate backdrop of twilight which coloured all dreaming.

The unicorn slept at the bottom of Ariel, between the roots on a nest of leaves. Even when she was too large to curl up in the womblike hollow she slept beneath the tree. She was most content and when winter came, covering everything with a white blanket, there was no difference between Maia and the landscape. She drank the snow and lived on acorns found in plenty below her guardian

6

oaks. There were places where the snow could not reach because the branches were so massive and these dry, kind spaces were the unicorn's larder and bed.

She could sense yuletide coming. Everything in the surrounding countryside seemed brighter and clearer. The air, cleansed by the fields of fresh snow, was as pure as mountain air. Now snowflakes had fallen in great dancing cascades from evaporating clouds, the sky was free again from its prison, and the calmest blue imaginable. The large, iridescent eyes of the unicorn reflected the sky, and the snow, and the knobbly outlines of the oaks.

On Christmas Eve she was awoken by the sound of tiny leather boots disturbing the twigs. Gnomes were decorating the branches with the most fragile and gayest of ornaments. Pieces of glass of every colour imaginable, as fine as icicles, hung on silver threads. Little gnarled men with hands as rough and tough as bark, worked

7

speedily but carefully, pipes in their mouths and a gleam in their compassionate brown eyes. There were dozens of them bearing garlands, and ladders that they perched on branches. They carried lanterns holding candles, to light when the evening of Christmas Eve came with awesome holiness. Maia knew at this time of the year Heaven was nearer to the Earth, and angels were close by rejoicing.

The sky was extremely clear on Christmas Eve. The unicorn watched entranced as sunset transformed everything into an amazing vision.

Pale pink snow folded the fields into silken sheets. The stars appeared from some elusive place where they had been hiding all day and the unicorn gazed up from her soft bed of leaves, up through the branches of the decorated oak, connecting with realms

8

many dreams away. Everything shimmered. Every creature, of whatever size or intelligence, was filled with heavenly light.

Then Maia slept for it was midnight.

She dreamt an angel was standing in the snow radiating beams of light. The angel sang a carol so sweet and gentle that the unicorn, even though she slept, felt the notes penetrating her heart. Then the fields were full of angels playing snowballs and chasing the unicorn through the deep drifts. But she ran faster than all of them.

Christmas morning dawned with a million dreams. In country churches stained glass angels watched over the birth of Jesus, and the scent of Christmas trees blended with incense. The smoky odour of midnight mass candles still pervaded the silence with whispered prayers from the lips of small children clutching toys, discovered at the bottom of their beds during the night.

Bells rang out over the snowy fields and Maia awoke to find a present beside her on a little pile of white feathers. The gift, wrapped in gold and silver paper, was tied with a red ribbon. The unicorn carefully pulled it open with her teeth. Inside the prettily engraved silver box was a magical quartz crystal. Maia gazed and gazed at the crystal. Curious winter sunlight cut through the branches and through the crystal. Rainbow colours trembled on the snow.

For an entire day the world stopped. Peace clung to the countryside in a fine vapour. The unicorn's heart overflowed with happiness, like a Christmas stocking bursting with surprises. The oaks stood perfectly still, wearing decorations sunbeams turned into jewels. This day was perfect, as was every other day. But this, the Christ Mass, revealed a higher degree of perfection. The celestial presence of angels filled the atmosphere as blissfully as snowflakes.

A massive red candle, standing on moss, was lit in a clearing. The unicorn guarded the flame until it eventually flickered out on New Year's Day, leaving a small angel of wax.

Spring brought renewal after the long, deathlike sleep, the Creation bursting again from the mystical womb where it had been nurtured and regenerated. Maia could feel the movement beneath

12

the ground as it broke open in ecstasy, when the wind changed direction and blew back the migrant birds from the South. She danced on her hind legs beneath the oaks, a dance of joy, a dance of life. The music she heard came from the breeze rustling through the branches, examining the green shoots.

The colour of hope became a vivid green and spread across the landscape bringing primroses with moon-pale petals. And the gold of springtime glowed in clusters of daffodils every possible shade of yellow. They were attended by faeries, only visible if the unicorn concentrated very hard and tried not to blink or breathe. These butterfly creatures also cared for white and pink blossom spread in a mist across the trees and hedgerows – for snowdrops and bluebells – for rhododendrons and camellias leaping up in clearings in exotic pale pink and gorgeous red fountains.

13

Maia heard the music of the gypsies, the nomadic tribes, all those whose connection with the Mother had not been lost or broken. They continued to return to the source for renewal, an esoteric domain where all visions and dreams were held. Their energy did not come from food but was an invisible spiritual sustenance.

Spring made the unicorn restless. She studied the horizon and knew she had to take a journey. The quartz crystal beneath Ariel gleamed with such brilliance, spoke of places Maia needed to find, far away from the oaks that had witnessed her birth and then protected her like parents.

The unicorn wandered, each day went a little further, exploring the thickets and copses, shady groves only the Elementals knew. Hoping to find an answer, yet always returning at nightfall to the protective Oak Circle. Her sleek body shone in the moonlight as

14

she slept and dreamt and visited remote planets and planes of existence. Sleep was the most beautiful awakening.

The day dawned when she did not return. The crystal emitted powerful signals activating a force, calling her so gently yet persistently. She had wanted to go and yet wanted to stay. She resisted the tug of the Oak Circle. Change was inevitable and the most natural thing, for nothing in Nature remained still for a split second. Otherwise, everything would be a frozen image, a still life, a living death. This dilemma every soul faced. Going forward meant leaving behind so much. But the stir of a promise, a forgotten vow, prompted. Nothing was ever lost, simply locked safely in the memory of the Great Spirit.

So the unicorn resisted turning back. She had no idea where she would sleep that night. Her life had become a grand adventure now and she knew she had to pay attention for signs along the path. If she missed anything she would be truly lost.

May, most beautiful and vibrant of all the months, assisted the unicorn in her quest, propelling her forward with the same urge that caused towering horse chestnuts to burst into flame.

All along the hedgerows a celebration of blossom skipped in the breeze, warmer and more loving each new day. There was no room for doubt in her heart filled with longing and the need to solve a mystery, a puzzle. The clues were carefully pieced together in the starry sky. She lay gazing up at the stars as they flashed and burst and floated, filling her with deep peace and a sense of atonement. They spread their rays over her in a counterpane. She felt safe as they whispered her into sleep.

Sleep lifted her into another dimension. She left her white body on the soft ground, and drifted away into the luminescence

16

beckoning from above. She travelled upwards, a fine gauze carried in the ether as effortlessly as birds and butterflies make flight, inhaling stardust, the essence of all dreaming. When she awoke with the first blackbird notes she could not remember where she had been. It was as distant and intangible as the ancient Oak Circle waiting for her return.

Dreams travel through those who dream like blood travels through the body, unseen but the most essential part of the whole. For without dreams we are dead. Who is wise enough to separate the dream from the reality or the reality from the dream?

If dreams had given the unicorn clues she was not aware of them, but proceeded slowly, leaving a trail of delicate hoof prints. She allowed her heart to be open to signals. Sometimes, as fragile as early morning mist disappearing in the sunlight, she glimpsed an angel pointing the way.

17

Maia came at last to a huge, hollow oak. It stood in the middle of a field where the grass was as high as the unicorn's shoulders. Orange butterflies flew up in swarms as she disturbed their afternoon sleep. She poked her horn inside the hollow and felt around with her front hooves. Earth was moulded into steps that wound down into the roots. The unicorn entered fully, blending with the innermost thoughts of the tree.

Torches flared and flickered, illuminating the descent as the unicorn met her shadow, grotesque and changing, on the rough walls. She felt her way down cautiously, her sensitive hooves soundless. If all the torches had been suddenly blotted out by a mischievous breath of wind her shimmering horn would have acted as her lantern.

The steps spiralled round and down, so deep into the ground it was easy to forget the sky existed. Down and down and further

18

down. The unicorn's heart beat as sweetly as a drum made of the finest and strongest skin. She descended in a trance, hypnotised, intoxicated by the intimacy of creation. A warm, mossy, highly sensuous perfume filled her lungs and sang through her body.

After what seemed aeons and no time at all, Maia discovered a doorway, slightly ajar. An alluring radiance filtered from inside. The unicorn nudged the heavy door open until there was sufficient space to slip through into a passage, also lit by flaring torches. She crept through a low archway.

In the centre of an ornate chamber she gazed upon the magnificent Crystal Skull mounted on a plinth of purest silver. The dazzling Skull emitted arcs of light. The unicorn curtsied, bending her little front legs in homage – genuflecting, her horn sweeping against the crystal-studded floor. The power in the chamber was immense, overwhelming. Only because of her incredible purity could Maia bare herself to this illumining.

As she gazed in awe, archangels on either side of the Skull became visible, rising up endlessly. Wings intricate spectrums of feathers, golden auras tinted with silver. Their faces had such divine expression, any being who glanced into their loving eyes would feel a heart expansion. The angel on the right wore a cloak of deepest blue, twinkling with stars, and the other a cloak of passionate red from which small winged creatures emerged, tiny humming birds, dragonflies and honey bees.

22

A UNICORN DANCED IN THE WOODS

Maia had been summoned to the Skull as animals are called to migrate by forces immensely dynamic and instinctive, from mystical places where the finest dreams, and sunrises and sunsets are painted. She slept, head on hooves, the crystal floor programming her body with sheer luminescence. The unicorn rose in a vapour through the night sky, like a whisper.

Maia felt herself being drawn into the spell of the dreaming Moon. The Queen of Dreams waited, silvery white and regal, holding a huge mirror for her to gaze into. She touched the surface with her muzzle and the Moon shattered. Now Maia was passing through the mirror, to all other planets in the solar system. From the Moon, Earth looked like a tiny marble. Streams of stars flowed. The unicorn could hear their silence in the ultimate miracle of the night sky.

She flew from planet to planet, using a higher sense to project her soul into each different atmosphere. Within every orb she discovered an awesome Crystal Skull. The crystalline intelligence held the cosmos together. The Moon is the Queen of Dreams and through her Maia dreamt the solar system. Each planet projected its vibration to mix with the energies of the others, making everything unique. Fire of Mars blended with love of Venus, speed of Mercury, discipline of Saturn, mystery of Pluto, gaiety of Jupiter, vulnerability of Chiron, revolution of Uranus, depth of Neptune. They resonated with the cosmic orchestra. The Sun, mightiest, and around which all circled.

The night sky was a complex map. Great mystical beasts spun in diamonds. The unicorn's heart a star pulsating with light spreading out through her aura as she slept and dreamt so deeply the dream within a dream within a dream. Astrology of time

26

transmuted into eternity and the dream moment was forever and forever.

The unicorn slept as if in meditation. The Moon wrapped Maia in her beams and slowed the Sun, so that darkness hesitated. Out of the darkness all things came.

When Maia woke she was back in the chamber of Earth's Crystal Skull. The archangels had watched over her dainty body, waiting for her soul to return from the long journey. Then, she slept again, even more soundly and awoke inside another dream, comfortingly familiar as she gazed up and saw the branches of Ariel, the gigantic oak, embracing the sky.

It was now Midsummer and the tree was a stage for all sorts of wildlife. Leaves fluttered and the Sun drew perfume from the grass which mingled with the perfume of every living creature, tree, and

27

plant. A golden haze clung to the landscape where waves of heat shimmered. Wild flowers tripped across the meadows and already the promise of berries hung in hedges where very small beasts sought shelter. A buzzing, humming, and twittering, almost hysterical earlier in the day, virtually silenced as the afternoon yawned and then snoozed.

When twilight came, flooding cornfields with tinted shades, the unicorn stretched and alerted herself. She sensed a movement towards her, the beating of a similar heart, felt the vibration she had unconsciously longed for. Everything in the universe seemed to hold its breath as the magnificent unicorn picked his way across the grass, mane spun from gold. His name was Endreol and he too had come to cast his spell.

There was a great celebration. The Elemental Kingdom arranged the wedding which took place a few days later beneath the trees.

28

Ribbons were twisted around branches. Elves, pixies and gnomes, picked and carried roses of many colours and fragrances, for the rose is truly the flower of love. Butterflies formed a wedding train. Hedgehogs, squirrels, rabbits, pheasants, and moorhens were bridesmaids and pages. Faeries were called forth on silver pipes played by tree elves. Badgers, foxes and deer were invited. Above everything floated a confetti of chanting birds.

A reclusive dragon attended.

Archangels filled the heavens with their blessings. The quartz crystal, found on Christmas morning, gleamed on top of the wedding cake created from herbs, petals and red currants. The Moon, who truly is the Queen of Dreams, hung in a fine crescent as the feasting began.

Maia and Endreol danced on their hind legs silhouetted against the deep orange sky, slowly disappearing into a sea of stars....

29

A UNICORN DANCED IN THE WOODS

Dream Again

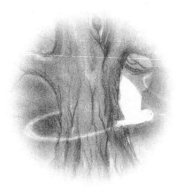

Valley of the Shadow

MOUNTAINS powdered with snow as pure as a unicorn, stretched up to the clouds that wrote indecipherable messages in the bluest sky. Mists became great cloaks under which these giants were suddenly invisible. Mirror lakes so still and clear everything turned upside down.

Maia could just about remember this land. She had stared at her own reflection and drunk the ice-cool water from countless waterfalls, jumping joyously over massive structures that stored the knowledge of the ages. Mountains spoke the language of silence, powerful beyond any form of speech or song. Maia felt alone here though other unicorns roamed and grazed. Stories of this homeland had been passed down. Many, like dreams, were almost forgotten.

At the base of the mountains were fast-running streams, singing as they tumbled over small rocks and boulders. And weeping rain forest trees, branches draped with moss and ferns, climbed as far as they could. The Standing People greeted the Stone People. These forests were as deep, mysterious, as healing as the lakes. Highest branches touched the stars and roots penetrated the darkness that gave life. Of the many lakes there was one lake special above all other and one mountain only the nimblest and lightest unicorn

34

could climb. They were nameless and there was no map with which to find them. Maia searched for a long time, trusting she would be guided to the right place, that her journey would not be wasted. Sometimes she was overcome with weariness as twilight fell over the enchanted landscape, bringing faraway stars into the sky.

She sheltered in caves and woke with the Sun that always brought hope with the newborn morning, melted the frost and warmed the dew. She nibbled wild strawberries, primroses, and mushrooms manifesting as part of an amazing conjuring trick. Maia was happy feeling the warmth around her and the playful air whispering through her long mane. And the journey became more meaningful, as the end of the path and hidden things beckoned.

Up in the giddiest heights where the glaciers stood carved and awesome (many eyes, many faces staring out, watching) the

35

unicorn climbed seeking secrets, her heartbeat echoing in the majestic spaces between rocks and clouds. The clouds floated low, casting shadows. Streams gushed from hidden places turning into pools of silver. Beads of moisture glistened on her gentle body.

One morning at dawn Maia discovered a vast lake as clear and still as a looking glass. The Morning Star lingering in the sky lay deep within, as had the full Moon hours earlier when all slept, guarded by the spirits of the night who awake in dreams and dance the future. Into the lake she shed her tears. Here was the place of shadow and of light. Carefully she dipped her curious hoof. The surface splintered into a thousand broken pieces, sparkling and rippling into spinning circles. Soft, cool fingers coaxed the unicorn in until she was suddenly uncomfortably out of her depth.

As she became immersed she saw the horses of the lake with their foaming manes and fathomless eyes. She was sinking yet galloping through the green satin of the lake, chasing memories or

36

the future. A tiny bubble of eternity that broke, melted, merged into the whole. Her rainbow tears had fallen upon the lake and fused with the one tear, the Element of Water, purifier and washer away of all sadness.

Maia absorbed the radiance left in the water by the Moon and the Morning Star. She led the lake horses to the shore and into the forest. They shook themselves and tiny jewels of the lake flew sparkling in the Sun, caught on the branches of meditating trees. Deep into the forest she ventured, her sleek form brushing against the bark of trees so tall it was impossible to glimpse the top branches or even imagine how high they grew. Each tree carried its own legend. Each tree watched Maia as she picked her way through the dense growth where the Sun sent shafts of gold.

Right in the centre an enormous fire blazed, dancing and curling and bursting. Maia heard Fire talking, crackling, laughing,

37

simmering and exploding. When the darkness came she curled up in his warm embrace and fell into a deep, contented sleep. Fire guarded her from violence and intrusion, softly went to sleep himself under the stars that burn with ice fire.

In her sleep Maia travelled up to the great map of light charting the heavens, where the Wheel of the Zodiac circles time. Here were all kinds of beasts, shining and shimmering in the night sky. Here time was measured and converted to stardust. The Bull, the Crab, the Lion, the Fishes, the Scorpion, and the Goat glistened like diamonds. All ever known and will be known written in powerful symbols, ruling night and all secrets.

Far beyond these wondrous constellations Maia travelled, further than the North Star and the Southern Cross, where the Plough no longer furrows through the darkness, where the Great

Unicorn is marked out, his horn like a compass pointing towards the Creator – always invisible, though visible in the Creation.

There she waited for messages, for inspiration, to hear the voice that spoke so mysteriously within the profound silence held together by each twinkling star. An endless tapestry of flickering candles to show the way to sailors, night fliers, and swimmers of the deep.

Cocooned in the velvet of the cosmos Maia felt the heartbeat of the huge beast. With each beat, brilliance shimmered through him and floated away as a fine, swirling mist, gradually evaporating. Then she heard the message clear as a church bell on a still morning – to trust, TRUST. She fell back from where she had been dreaming, galloping with the King on the Great Unicorn Plain, her mane a thousand stars and her hooves gleaming with silver dust.

Maia was awoken by a rustling that made everything around her quiver. It grew and expanded, breathing, stirring, pulling, tearing, so that every creature, however large or small, became afraid, wanted to run away but could not escape. The Great Wind came from all directions, caused confusion, blowing dead leaves up into swirling tornadoes, transporting objects that had no intention of moving, many miles. Maia held on, drowning in sound waves and the screams of falling trees dying.

42

The Element of Air demanded respect. When he spoke his voice grew into a wild concerto, carried many nuances. When he was still he appeared to disappear. This was illusion for without the breath that healed, cleansed, and regenerated there was no life. The winds that blew from the North and the East carried snow and fear. The winds from the South and West were comforting and mellow. The South Wind, especially playful, swirled with birds and butterflies. The West Wind blew towards old age and death. But this was an enlightened place and the natural end of the cycle.

The West was where it was possible to look back with joy or regret. Here darkness came eventually but also promises of the most glorious sunset. Here was where the tribal ancestors sat cross-legged on Mother Earth and made their connection. Their multi-coloured, feathered garments lifted them into higher realms.

43

Maia held on somehow, when there was nothing to hold on to. She dug her hooves deep and tried to remember stillness and peace. The Great Wind pulled her away from the ground, picking her up with an arm of ether which forced her to fly. And the pain she had expected turned into ecstasy as she floated like a feather. Holding on was not the way to survive but to flow as streams and rivers, gushing and exploding, cascading free fall over rocks. The Elements created change, supreme miracle of the Creation. Nothing stayed still, nothing was meant to. The seasons greeted each other with such passion. Spring was a little child and Winter a wise warrior.

When the winds ceased, she grazed on the calm plains watching the clouds form into mountains, gods, demons, and angels. There were pinnacles and sky lakes sunset turned to crimson, gold – and when darkness fell, became only what Maia remembered.

44

Each morning she frolicked over the lovely homeland, kicking up her heels, rolling in the velvet grass embroidered with daisies, forget-me-nots, buttercups, and love-in-the-mist.

She pretended to touch the clouds with her hooves, reaching out for what is untouchable and unknowable. Here was the nearest place to knowing, to insight.

She was alone but complete, just as everything around her was complete with its own song, pattern, and weave. The trick was to merge and to feel detached. When she had exhausted herself grazing, dancing and wandering, she slept under the low-hanging, protective branches at the base of a pine. Dreams came.

Maia dreamt of the Earth Mother from whose great womb everything emerged, where everything died. The Mother opened her tender arms, took all back into herself, and gently grieved. This grieving, although necessary, did not last long. In hardly any time that which had fallen apart, to pieces, formed into new life, having merged and found energy to rebirth as the love flowed back. The

47

tiniest fragment mattered for without these countless fragments there would have been nothing.

The Mother wore an unimaginably beautiful gown, laced with great rivers and valleys. A vast cloak that held all trees and flight of eagles, flowed around her. Fur of the wolf, bear, and lion trimmed this garment, magnificent feathers from humming birds, and wings of dragonflies. Mother Earth gazed at her ever-changing image mirrored by the sea, and sang the Song of the Heart. Her gown was woven from the glistening yarn of spiders, discarded skin of snake, bats' hooks, fur of cat, light of glow-worm.

Her cloak carried the scent of acorns, fallen leaves, honeysuckle and the divine, intoxicating perfume of the rose, the earthy fragrance of freshly arisen mole hills, and lavender. The amazing cloak spun around, rippling when the winds caught it,

48

coveting the inexpressibly fine trinkets the Earth Mother stored in her jewel case – opals, gold, diamonds, amethyst and the rose quartz of love. All that sparkled and glittered like eyes shining with happiness. Silver, the ores fashioned into weapons for unconquerable knights.

All this the Mother held.

She also held the tiny seeds that burst forth into sweeping fields of grain, seeds that become apples, blackberries, delicious wild fruits, hips, and pods. She held these and the feathery clocks of dandelions which explode, drift, try to tell time. Her treasure troves overflowed, were endless and always filled with more surprises. Miracles, tricks, gifts, magic. Skin of toad, breast of penguin, eye of the fox, shadow of deer, wild horses charging in a sea of energy. All that rested and never moved, waiting with sticky nets, hungry

49

mouths, in dark, dank places. Innocent and preyed upon; scorpion stinging itself to death; blind worms and skylarks.

She held all this and much more.

And when she breathed deeply and her mood changed, everything moved with her. Clouds skipped. Trees bent. Waves reached for the sky, fell defeated into a snow of foam, and tried again. When the Mother moved, when the Mother turned in her sleep or awoke from the deepest dream, then - like a huge, multi-coloured Mexican quilt - fields, forests, meadows, lakes, streams, ponds, ditches, pools, and hills were rearranged. When her calm and tranquillity turned to rage, mountains rumbled and volcanoes exploded. Streams of lava became seething torrents, reshaping and remoulding her ancient body. Above the Moon sailed, controlling tides and the moods of women.

50

So many moods, essences, unwritten languages, a bringing together and pulling apart, never quite still, always waiting, always evolving. The Mother cared for all, especially the unicorn called Maia. She studied her with pride as she stood quivering on the edge of the horizon listening to the eternal stillness and tuning in. She had cradled and nursed her, experienced yet again the pain of knowing her children needed to be free.

Maia dreamed her way into the past and future, standing high on a hillside, gazing out at the sunset which flooded the plains with a soft sea of gentle tints. She linked with the Great Crystal Skull buried in the Earth. She recalled her journey from the Circle of Oaks with the small crystal to guide her, and her marriage to the unicorn Endreol, Prince of Magical Beasts, Keeper of the Truth and Shower of the Way. At first it was painful to remember but once she had opened the memory it was impossible to close.

After the wedding they had sought the homeland. They slept beneath the curious stars feeling the pulse of the Earth as they travelled through the universe. Each dream trip took them further and further away. On the eleventh planet Chiron – Wounded Warrior who heals himself through healing others – difficulties had arisen. Maia felt his wound pierce her heart like a lance. The agony seared through her delicate body, weakened by the pain and sorrow of humanity, all creatures that had ever lived.

Chiron was the planet of emotions, unmet needs, the wound of wounds floating through the ether like a fantastic Maori canoe. It cut through the ego as ruthlessly as a Samurai sword. The pain and pus had to leak out, the pain become conscious before the wound could heal. Hidden, unacknowledged wounds whispered.

Maia awoke, but Endreol did not return that night. He had completely disappeared. Although for many nights Maia sought him in her dreams there was never a glimpse of him. She often pondered on what might have happened to him for his powers were awesome. What could be so compelling to waylay this mighty creature?

Days dawned and dusked but Maia never ceased to believe Endreol would eventually return. They would walk together, watched by the stars and the Queen of Dreams who held the Earth spellbound. This loneliness would end. Hope was a heavy lantern but she acted as if it were the slightest burden, the lightest weight. Very far away she could sense Endreol's heartbeat throbbing through the cosmos, the endless web of twinkling stars around which every thought pulsated invisibly like an electric current.

On Chiron, Endreol had stumbled across his shadow, a huge beast shaped like a unicorn, with a massive horn and the blackest body. His eyes were dark as coals and when Endreol dared to look into them he froze with fear. He who had never known fear was suddenly petrified. As he travelled into the eyes of the monster, Endreol began to forget, to lose his identity. The eyes were like holes into which he fell until he reached the void. There he lay, his magnificent body wasting and fading.

Time ceased and the only way to measure was by decay. Not even the peace and stillness of the NOW could invade this limbo state. Although the unicorn's body appeared to be dead this was an illusion. His etheric body had taken over the struggle against the fiendish force, a negative mirror image coming from within his own heart.

He paced the gloomy caves that imprisoned him. The walls were covered in slime, and grotesquely masked bats hung down, their clammy wings teasing. Around his proud hooves snakes wove intricate knots. Spiders, which had never seen the light of day

55

or the Moon, were as thick as bracken. The saddest, most destructive thought forms pervaded the stale air - fears, restraints, inhibitions, denials, abuse, and torture. Particularly unholy spots were haunted by suicide, murder, despair.

Endreol tried to imagine the stars but the sickening stench, the negativity stifled him like a swamp in which he was drowning. Each step took him further and further out of his depth. At first he had been able to think of Maia, that kept him safe and focused. But after a while he was unable to remember she existed, and he was having difficulty in remembering even his own name. Maia dreamt shadow dreams. She rose on the nightmares to the scariest places. She searched without finding, her lantern held high, and a bright flame in her shrinking heart. She was determined not to let go of this frailest hope, this fragile link to her soul mate. She urged the mares on, challenging them to take her where only the foolish,

56

desperate, and those who loved would go. Her love made her stronger, although more vulnerable. The purity and directness of her feelings was powerful enough to take her where the lost and damned were trapped, without becoming trapped too. The Guardians came close, Raphael, Michael, and Gabriel, their boundless wings protecting her.

She returned to her waking state to restore and refresh herself before she journeyed out again on another nightmare. Nightmares were the opposite of daydreams, sometimes equally perilous. She wondered if Endreol had ceased to love her, had taken another path, started a new journey on which she did not belong. When such thoughts flashed into her mind she rejected them, although they stabbed at her like small, razor-sharp daggers. Faith, trust, patience, humility – the Crystal Skull had instructed her to practise these disciplines.

57

Endreol weakened. It was as if his blood had been drained by vampires. His body lay motionless, wilted, shrivelled, an unrecognisable life-dead thing, though still linked to his soul by a silver cord. His only hope now was to connect with an entity which vibrated with the same energy of all that he had forgotten and lost.

He was half-asleep and calm, having reached the Valley of the Shadow where the light filtered over the hillsides awakening memories of what he had once been. When this faded, a brilliant star rose and he danced a kind of polka, a gypsy dance connecting his weary hooves again to the Great Mother. As he danced Endreol was aware of many changes. He summoned up the rhythm, the mystical pounding beat that is the Dance of Life.

Then he was flying in ever-widening circles and cycles, faster than speed, brighter than light. His mane and tail flowed as he moved ecstatically, merging with the Elements he was part of and

58

were part of him. Earth to ground; Air to deepen mind, giver of knowledge and wisdom; Water to heal wounds, wash away fear, end grief, and restore trust and innocence. Fire to stir him burning into joy, to become illuminated and enlightened. When all four Elements were balanced and he was poised in the centre of the Medicine Wheel, he shone and was free.

It was then that he noticed Maia, a few paces away in a clearing between the aged oaks. The early evening sky was deep orange with traces of twilight pink. Branches were silhouetted against the meadow where rabbits played hide-and-seek and evening birds skimmed and soared in flight rhythms that slowed everything down. Their notes rang across the fields with a mellow resonance.

The evensong was sung and butterflies disappeared. All creatures closed their eyes and woke in places forgotten during the day. The long grass swished as Endreol moved towards the clearing, hardly able to remember a fragment of what he had experienced in the dark place. It was as if he had awoken from a dream which fell apart and evaporated like mist over an expanse of water when the Sun comes up. His wound had healed and the healing had taken many circles of the Sun. Now he walked out of the wound like the brave warrior he was, clear of all wounds and stronger.

Maia had waited patiently and was rewarded. She was stronger too.

They stood side by side in the Circle of Oaks, finely etched against the radiant sky which fell behind the trees in the most exquisite sheet of silk.........

Dream More

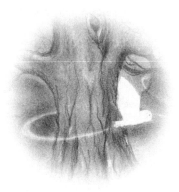

Tomorrow Is Yesterday

THROUGH the corridors of time Maia wandered, twisting and turning, seeking, often standing still, sometimes appearing to move backwards. This was the maze with the dragon in the centre and the dragon was a fantastically powerful but iillusory creature. As soon as he was seen he disappeared. Those who felt his fiery breath were scorched for many centuries.

65

But the dragon led the parade and insisted on being followed. And those who dared not go, who feared to dance faster and faster until they were flying, became lost in the labyrinth that had many dark corners and impassable spaces. The Maze of Eternity was a challenging place, with signposts and journeys in every direction. The paths were high or low, fast, slow, complex, simple. And all the time the heart's desire beckoned, promising fulfilment, ecstasy, and peace beyond measure.

The Path with Heart was the one to choose, after the thorns and shadows of fear were pushed out of the way. The Path with Heart led to happiness and the ever-present Now. This was the sacred realm where the light was held by radiant beings with multi-coloured wings and faces of astonishing purity. Their eyes brimmed with love which transformed those whose eyes reflected such a gaze. Every heart expanded on the Path with Heart and total joy was experienced.

66

In the early morning mist of autumn, the most alluring and enveloping of all mists – full of summer and dense as forgetfulness – spiders swam in the dew, and plants and long grass drank thirstily. Blackberries fattened. The harvest time was coming when golden wheat was bound into sheaves on ancient stone altars, in cool places that echoed; where prayers were sent to Heaven; where incense smouldered and candles danced. Mother Nature and God were one in a sensuous wedding which aroused, embraced, and fulfilled.

Crimson apples, giant marrows, gourds of all the yellows and oranges of October. Sweetcorn, chrysanthemums filling the ether with the earthiest and most pungent aroma. This was the time of the acorn, of the falling leaf. A time for squirrels to store passionately and for winter larders to be dug by long-clawed badgers in a sea of soil.

67

Medieval tapestries, carved stone ravens of long-dead kings.

Birds were beginning to fly away on the wind like leaves scattering, and crows swaggered across the stubble. When the mists lifted as instantly as theatre curtains, scenes of warm beauty were revealed. Trees changing to match the season and the green of the heart chakra becoming rich gold, brown, orange, and maroon. It was a celebration of the Sun, a ripening and enriching, a time of deep passion, a song which could be seen.

A UNICORN DANCED IN THE WOODS

The smell of steaming soil and smouldering bonfires mingled and travelled over the fields and into the unreachable arms of tomorrow. And where was yesterday, and the things that had been, the past? Maia stood between the two in the place of timelessness, where all became clear like a landscape viewed from a hill. Timelessness was where all things came from and where all things went, visions within which the unicorn moved freely, without the slightest effort. She was able to go backwards, forwards, up and down, to the centre of the Earth or the outreaches of the universe. It was possible to be everywhere and anywhere. On her flowing mane the stardust gathered and sparkled as she moved. This was a new kind of measurement, Time of the Unicorn.

Maia pawed the long grass with her front hooves, the spirit of the horse raced through her blood. Her body had evolved from horse, giving speed and strength. From goat came nimbleness and agility. Both danced in her and with her. Energy of the swift horse and endurance of the climbing goat, moving towards elusive pinnacles, able to tackle, without fear, the roughest and most inhospitable terrain. The essence that passed through her was from both these four-legged creatures, while her unicorn soul came from the higher temples. Yet she was like a child in the meadow of her life, chasing dragonflies and formless dreams.

Moonset and sunrise, sunset and moonrise, highway of stars were the measure of her being. Sometimes her horn caught in gossamer spiders' webs dusty with autumn. She smelt of hay, dry leaves, and dying flowers. Winter was as far away as death. Rabbit holes were busy and butterflies drank nectar from flowers indistinguishable from their wings. But when the Great Wind came with his brothers, all would be blown to the place of memory holding every fragment of all that has ever been.

71

When the winds came Maia stood firm against the horizon, her mane and tail dancing. She was not afraid of change. She welcomed the crispness in the air, the need to become more alert. It was so quiet and calm after the winds blew themselves out. The Sun dried the branches of giant oaks penetrated by gusts as sharp as knives. They had waltzed wildly, night after night, in the bold arms of their lovers, who came as unexpectedly as they left.

The ground beneath the oaks was scattered with acorns and the trees could see the unicorn passing below. All was quieter and slower for the winds had frightened away many insects and small animals and birds. It was time of the robin and the prowling cat, foxes. Horses stood sleeping in frost-bound fields until the stars set and the Sun created for the dawn the most gorgeous garment. The journey was more difficult when winter came for the spirit was forced inside and all creatures were faced with limitations of self,

73

unless they slept and hibernated. On sunny days, when the still oaks awoke from their slumber for a few hours and stretched in the warmth, the unicorns basked in the golden light. And their steps became trots as they cantered out into the sleeping fields that yawned, turned over, and went back to sleep. Underground much was happening and all hibernating creatures dreamt the long, dark mysterious sleep of winter. Endreol and Maia slept beneath the oaks sharing the trees' dreams.

Dream of the oak went deep, deep into the Earth, winding and curving to haunts of toad and worm and snake and centipede, stag beetle and rolled hedgehog. While in the branches the owl dreamt with creeping insects still as stone. Restless squirrels performed spectacular trapeze acts.

The heart of the oak was ginormous and immensely loving.

74

Each day the energy changed, slowed, and pulled back and inwards. The setting sun became blood-red and sank over an intricate weave of leafless branches, linked across the luminous sky waiting for the stars to drop down. The Sun was weaker, dying, yet was still empowered. Maia and Endreol often stood bathed in the sunset, absorbing the colours and watching entranced until the darkness came. There was beauty in the darkness too, for it was soft, gentle, and calming.

The night creatures became busy, stimulated by moonbeams, feared because they were enigmatic and unpredictable. But it was they that were the most sensitive and fearful. The unicorns were able to cross the barrier between day and night. They had depth and clarity, were not intimidated by extremes of light or dark, held nothing they wished to hide.

75

Around Christmas there was a period of total stillness when biting frost petrified soil, corn stalks, snoozing hedges, empty snail shells, discarded skin of slow-worm. The grass crunched as the unicorns picked their way warily through the shimmering landscape to ponds rigid with ice. In the rarefied serenity the yuletide Sun turned everything it touched to gold leaf.

This sacred period of the year had always been special, even in the most ancient days reaching back beyond any record or memory. It was time of the mistletoe. Death and rebirth were celebrated passionately in hidden churches truly part of the living landscape. The stonework of these churches was a breathing, feeling body. Inside, candlelight shone on brass vessels, cast wavering shadows on December-cold flagstones, beneath which knights and their ladies were buried and who still held hands. Not many clock turns after, a child named Spring came forth from this wedding of holly, and danced barefoot in the glades.

Maia and Endreol had been through aeons, manifesting and disappearing as centuries rolled by. Always they found each other, sometimes after gargantuan challenges and struggles. They rode the karmic wheel with all Creation.

The Wheel of Fortune rose and fell. Kings became beggars, saints murderers, children old. The wheel turned as Earth turns, and all the planets, for everything is part of an endless cycle. The stone circles from prehistoric days, sunken like neglected graves, yearned to come alive again and manifest the power they held. Ignored, misunderstood, they also held pain, and with aged trees waited for closed hearts to open.

Maia and Endreol danced the stone circles, stared into the circles in each other's eyes and the opening to other worlds and

77

dimensions. Gilded spiral staircases leading down, around and upwards. They danced the gypsy dances that awoke the Earth from her dream.

The unicorns wandered and then rested. Each place had its own individual vibration and language. This was the most beautiful, sensuous Earth dream. The heady perfumes the Mother exuded were overpowering. Stillness was as meaningful as dancing. When they were still Maia and Endreol expanded like white clouds, appearing to be motionless as they floated, but always subtly changing, dispersing, and reinventing themselves.

The key to the future was buried deeply with all the karma of the ages. There had been a time when the Mother had been childless, only the Elements had existed. She played with Fire, Wind, and Water. The seas formed and the massive continents were moulded.

78

Flashes of lightning had crackled through forests where the secrets of eternity were hidden. The Mother was lonely and needed to be seen, for her womb to be full. From her came all wild beasts, insects, fish, and birds. Then the Soul Children with their shining auras and rainbow eyes, journeyed from the stars. The Mother was happy. The stars were linked together by starlight. But gradually the Soul Children began to forget where they had come from. Their auras faded like flower petals and the Ancient Wisdom they had brought with them was lost.

The dragon lay dying, turning into a mountain of bones and crumbling scales. There was no one to believe in him and without belief the most potent dream is extinguished, as sadly as a solitary flame in the darkness. Dreamless sleep and dreamless waking bound the Earth like a cruel lover who controls by withholding and forces the love back inside the unloved, where it either dies or turns

79

to hate. But Mother Earth loved unconditionally. She gave, and patiently, and sometimes a little sadly, waited for her generosity to be reciprocated. She saw all of history come and go. It was but a single heartbeat.

The Great Council of Twelve was summoned and met in the Circle of Oaks where Maia had first danced with ecstasy. Enigmatic figures clad in white robes, hooded, heads bowed, their auras spreading out over the fragrant grass carpets their feet hardly seemed to touch.

Maia and Endreol watched from a distance, alert and shimmering. The strangers had appeared through a gap between the oaks. One followed the other in a flowing procession, dignified and purposeful. They carried lanterns, not yet lit, for it was noon and the Sun was high in the sky and there were no shadows or dark places. As they made their way an ethereal vibration penetrated the

80

atmosphere, hushing bird song and insect hum. A stood-stillness came with them like the pause before the beginning of a great prayer.

One by one they formed into a circle and pulled the hoods from their heads. Every face shone with ageless beauty, a perfect blend of masculine and feminine. Their eyes were direct and compassionate. Each carried a scroll containing part of the Ancient Wisdom. They placed the scrolls in a pile and then sat on the ground with spines erect and began to meditate. As they meditated the colours surrounding them changed softly, from deep red, to orange, yellow, green, blue, indigo, and violet. Then a sudden surge of brilliant white light lifted them off the ground so that they were floating. They vibrated so fast that one moment they were there and in the blink of an eye had disappeared and reappeared.

81

They had come to the Oak Circle to change time, to readjust the spinning and spiralling. The Ancient Wisdom could only be entrusted to those who could detach from time and from their karma. Karma was like a complex web that had to be dispelled and blown away in the wind.

As they meditated the colours spread through the branches of the oaks into the Earth and up into the sky to the clouds. Every being was able to absorb them, find clarity and peace. Like a swarm of butterflies the colours shimmered and floated.

The insects and animals were aware of the new vibration and although they were woven into a strict pattern, an instinct which they always must obey, even they had a deeper sense of their beauty and there was a joy in the soaring of the birds, missing before. Worms wriggled through the soil with intimacy and small

82

beings shone. Tiny flowers were cosmic. For all is one and they were all part of the Mother's lovely gown.

All afternoon the seers sat in the circle, greatly at peace, greatly wise. They spoke to each other through their eyes. Their lips remained silent, for words could not express fully the feelings that emanated from their hearts. The pause between words was always where the real meaning fell.

Late in the afternoon the sages broke the circle and gathered up the parchment scrolls. One by one they read aloud the holy words like a benediction. One by one they rolled the scrolls and tied them with silver and gold thread.

When the Ancient Wisdom had been released into the ether they beckoned the unicorns to come and dance in the centre of the Oak Circle. They danced too, faster and faster, until they were a ring of white light floating away. They left the scrolls behind under the mighty oak Ariel.

The unicorns danced in the twilight, dissolving into mysterious landscapes where cloud unicorns were also dancing.

Maia and Endreol guarded the scrolls and waited. Although many days came and went they were perfectly content to be and wait.

Seasons merged. The oaks stood bare and stark. Then buds appeared and green shoots. Soon the trees were garlanded by whispering leaves giving shade and shelter. When the leaves fell slowly in burnished showers, the unicorns frolicked in the dry, rustling drifts piled around the sturdy roots.

Each moment there was a small miracle to behold, buzzing and bending, shaping and reforming. Something dying and yet

84

something being born. Acrobatic spiders spinning webs and busy birds building nests, small homes everywhere, beneath damp stones or fragile blades of grass. Frogs jumped and toads croaked. Slimy, unnamed creatures sought some kind of identity.

The time of the snow was the most dazzlingly beautiful for the light was intense. The unicorns, frozen in wonder as they gazed at the sparkling branches and jewelled icicles, could easily have been mistaken for unicorns of snow. What was time but one single moment, stretching out like a note that instead of fading grew louder? A seeding, a fixing and holding of fantastic works of art called dreams. Maia and Endreol were part of the dreaming and their own dreams were part of the alchemy.

They protected the scrolls from the snow, and when Spring came, timid and playful, they unrolled them and placed them in the Sun.

85

The lettering was intricate and of a long-forgotten language.....

Dream Sweetly

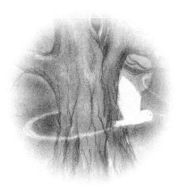

The Travelling Circus

WHEN the oaks were most shady the travelling circus began to appear through a gap in the hedgerow. Right in the centre of the Oak Circle a blue, green, and white striped tent was erected on huge poles, and sweet-smelling sawdust sprinkled from sacks by little men. Wagons pulled by white horses were decorated with carved, gold leaf scrolls. The circus had come from the dawn and would disappear into twilight. The circus was on a perpetual mystical journey, sequined and ethereal, woven from illusion and mystery, bursting with surprises.

Those who travelled with it had been specially chosen. Their talents were incredible and they were able to reach unreachable perfection. They felt the power of the trees and added their own power. The wagons formed a circle inside the Oak Circle, under the sparkling diamanté Big Top of the night sky.

Maia and Endreol hid behind the oak trees and waited for night to silence the sacred space where the wagons glistened in the moonlight. The fires had died down but the smell of the smouldering oak still lingered. Horses munched grass, becoming silver shadows. The only other animals the circus kept were dogs, now sleeping beneath the wagons. These dogs could dance on their

hind legs like the unicorns.

As the Sun rose, the doors of the dew-soaked wagons were unlatched to allow in the light and the earth-fragrant air. Clowns, conjurors, and acrobats yawned and stretched like exotic flowers opening their petals. They smiled at each other and regarded everything around them with eyes as sharp as razors. They also listened. No change in the sky went unnoticed. The softest bird note was distinguished from all others.

The gypsy blood raced through their veins, thick and dark red, on fire, centuries old, and seasoned like the finest wine. This was the blood of life, of the flamenco and fast-played violins and guitar chords that stirred love, longing, and deepest desire.

All through the day they practised the circus arts, defying gravity with their skills and allowing the human frame to become completely fluid. The musicians sat under the trees with their guitars, pipes and drums, with satin scarves around their heads,

93

ornate crucifixes at their throats and gold hoops in their ears. Many rings were on their sensitive fingers and their eyes flashed and gleamed like jewels.

The white horses were let loose in the surrounding fields to graze under the Midsummer sky, hazy with warmth and languid birds whose tricks were breathtaking.

At midday the circus folk paused from their practice. All sat on the ground around an enormous red and white checked tablecloth. They picnicked on huge, tangy cheeses, tomatoes, hardly bigger than marbles, bursting with sweetness. Hunks of newly baked bread were thickly spread with bright yellow butter and strawberry jam from fields picked in the late afternoon when the soil was warm. Crystal-clear water was handed around in earthenware goblets. Their smiles were wise and their eyes brimming with happiness.

94

Afternoon wore on, the shadows of the Oak Circle lengthening, flowing across the grass like ink. Evening birds began to call each other and the Sun slowly slipped away behind the hedgerows leaving strands of gold.

But it was light till very late. The air was balmy and softly embracing. Flares were carried inside the tent and when it was dusk the show began.

People had appeared to take their places on the wooden seating encircling the ring. An Egyptian high priestess waited expectantly with a medieval king and queen, knights, minstrels, barefoot children. Those from down the centuries, proud and humble, all seeking the same magic potion.

There were many acts. Each waited hidden in the shadows to run into the shining circle as out into the Sun. The dazzling colours

95

and vibrant music stirred reveries. Clowns masked sadness. The wire walker taunted fear. The sword swallower swallowed all pain. Fire eaters filled their mouths with flames as heroically as dragons.

Contortionist, juggler, fliers, weavers of illusion….

Far below the upturned faces responded to every nuance. The wire walker without safety net, intrepid, in perfect equilibrium, stepped out in pumps as light as thistledown. Hearts stopped, opened. He jumped above the wire, floating. He turned pirouettes in the air, somersaulted, sparkled.

The trapeze artist, holding on to a silver swing with one foot, golden hair flying; snake charmer; knife thrower; the lady rider jumping from horse to horse in her tutu; tumblers; strong man with oiled muscles, who could lift the world on his back.

The ringmaster wore a wonderful curled and powdered wig and a bright pink regency coat embroidered with flowers, the sleeves edged with lace. His high boots were of leather as soft as peach skin. His charisma kept everything under absolute control without a whip or apparently the slightest effort.

His wise eyes danced like the torches that lit the ring. His firm mouth was always about to break into a smile for he was amused by everything he saw. He knew that seeing is believing and what you believe comes true. He entered fully into the dream of the day and the dream of the night. The circus was one of his favourite dreams, a creation as fragile and delicate as a moth.

He bowed, acknowledged the excited audience who cheered as each new act brought higher levels of ecstasy and exhilaration. The escapologist untangled his chains. The woman sawn in half walked

97

whole from the ring. The magician from whose top hat a hundred doves flew. The clown skipping on stilts.

Maia and Endreol had stayed hidden all day but their curiosity was so extreme that they were irresistibly drawn to the glowing tent.

"And now," announced the ringmaster. "The act you have all been waiting for, *the Dancing Unicorns*!"

An outbreak of applause propelled Maia and Endreol to the centre of the ring. Together they danced, nimble and proud on their hind legs, the gypsy fiddler forcing them to move faster and faster until their bodies had entirely disappeared and they were two shafts of dazzling white light. Then they merged together into a huge shining ball that spread over the audience and the performers. This light was so intense that it pulled and drew everything inside. Even the tent disappeared into the luminous sphere, with the entire audience and the acts. Then, in the blink of an eye, all appeared just as before, a pulsating mass of colour and excitement.

Maia and Endreol bowed graciously out of the tent. How bright the stars were. They seemed to be caught in the branches of the trees, shooting and sparking. The massive oaks stood silently in the starshine, Great Beings whose thoughts stretched out into the night.

100

This was high summer when everything is at its fullest, when the heart of the rose bursts open with love, and honeysuckle twines. Season of flowering and opening. The unicorns roamed through the long grass. The Earth's heart pulsed beneath their hooves and vibrated through their bodies. In the distance the circus tent was silhouetted against the purple sky and in the morning would have vanished like a face from a mirror.

At dawn the travelling circus began to move away in the mist. The freedom-loving horses gracefully pulled wagons that rumbled like distant thunder. The eye-catching procession wound along the early morning lanes, twisting, turning, growing smaller and quieter. Maia and Endreol danced on their hind legs beneath the oaks, faster and faster, until they too were invisible....

So the circus travelled, arriving at far-flung commons, as welcome as a lovely surprise. When the twilight came and the glow-worms were visible, enticing music sought its way from the tent into the arms of trees. Excitement began to swell up from all the roots dug deep into the soil. Underground creatures, badgers, moles and shiny beetles came nearer the surface. Those high above – skylarks, martins and swallows – skimmed over the tent. A communion began as the stirring became more frenzied and the music louder and even more spellbinding.

The unicorns had followed for many months, trotting through the ever-changing landscape and weather. The tent had been pitched on unknown beaches and virgin snow. Through the seasons they paraded, discovering fields of daffodils and crunchy autumn drifts. The cycle repeated over and over, just as the wagon wheels turned round and round.

Sometimes they pitched in the middle of woodland, in clearings surrounded by hundreds of wise old trees. Here the acrobats would practise their tricks, hanging upside down by their legs from high branches. They clambered right to the top of the tallest trees and gazed out across green summits within touching distance of clouds. This was the domain of the solitary eagle. The artists climbed nimbly down with mottled feathers stuck in their hair.

In the woods the circus gave its best performances, for the energy was potent and mysterious, and true magic abounded. Tiny elves with lanterns appeared and disappeared. Moon shadow wrapped the performers in the palest light, and the audience was entirely of faerie creatures.

Always the unicorns were the last to appear, so graceful and ethereal; they danced fear into love, dark into light. A hush fell over the woods when the performance had ended and the sleeping trees dreamt deeply and sweetly..........................

103

In every place they performed they left an essence that lifted the harmonic of all that existed. From beaches it penetrated into the sea as far down as ancient shipwrecks. And when they climbed up mountain tracks, where pines stood bravely on the edge of gaping precipices, the unicorns' pure resonance filtered into clouds.

The circus travelled North, South, East, and West, sailed to the tiniest islands. Through burning deserts and over ice landscapes it connected with the energy of the rising Sun and the stories of the Moon. Magnificent sunsets turned the tent to every colour imaginable, and the atmosphere inside was very finely woven. It circled the Earth Mother divinely.

The trapeze artist and wire walker became more daring. The clowns were funnier and the acrobats supple as rubber. Every performance pushed the boundaries further. What had been sheer perfection a few days earlier, became commonplace.

Sometimes they ventured into the dingiest areas where the trees could hardly hold up their branches because of the heaviness in the air. Dark birds nested, hovered like malignant thought forms. These were the hiding places of bats, and all which feared the light.

Bravely the tent men hammered in the pegs, defying their secret urge to run away, They went about their work in such a skilful, commanding manner that these intimidating entities slunk off into the tangled, primeval meadows, where not even the pluckiest rabbit or most foolish deer would venture. In these limbo regions the audiences were patchy. It was difficult to tell human from phantom, projection from what was real. Horned creatures with coal-black eyes sat nearest the ring waiting for tragedy, hoping to inspire errors of judgement and falls. But the performers were powerfully focused and when Maia and Endreol trotted over the sawdust this negativity miraculously dispersed. Everything around the tent was bathed in golden light, wafting out through the flaps and gently illuminating all it could find.

But deep within the unicorns' hearts there was now weariness and unrest. The oaks began calling, Ariel, Dorc, Swinbourne, and Someil. The white owl flew out searching for them. The calling grew more persistent and disturbing. They needed to return to the source for energy. Yet how could they escape this spell which had bound them for so long and the addiction of performing, of observing performances that lifted them into a different dimension, like meditation?

How to say goodbye to those who lived through their feelings, whose hearts were ardent and fully open? They were unable to say goodbye, so they left wordless and tearless, late one evening when there was a full Moon to light their way. They left without thought or sorrow for this would have hindered them.

Finding their way home was difficult. They had so eagerly followed and fallen in with the rhythm of the circus, had journeyed so far, so long, that finding their own rhythm again was extremely challenging.

They drew closer together as they trotted along the unfamiliar lanes watched by invisible eyes. Some of the trees were unfriendly and stand-offish. Some of the ground felt as if it would crumble, not support them. At other places roots and nettles grew up when they approached, to catch and trip them.

But they dreamt as they moved cautiously along and communicated with the Great Crystal Skull. They shared the same dream although dreaming separately. They were at the centre of the Earth, where the radiance of the Skull penetrated darkness, negativity, and hardened hearts blocked by fear. When this quintessence entered those who sought enlightenment, they felt

107

intense pain. But once they had dared pass through the trauma of rebirth they were much stronger. The unicorns had experienced the excruciating pain of this shard piercing their being many times, but knew it was the doorway to illumination and freedom. The Skull was like a candle in the darkest night of the soul. The unicorns' shadows grew enormous, as they approached the light, wavering and flickering.

Courageously they went forward, although they were exhausted. They nibbled greenery, drank from springs which suddenly bubbled up unexpectedly like hope. They slept hidden away in thickets where they were awoken at dawn by birds whose sweetness soothed them.

For many days they journeyed, following the Sun until it slid over the hills. Circle after circle, spinning and turning. They encountered other travellers. Some had faith and determination.

108

Many others had lost their way, wandered aimlessly. Maia and Endreol were careful not to become involved or halted. And those who saw them pass were only aware of an essence, a shimmering, a hint of what they too could be.

The great fall of autumn came, when leaves drop like flames, forming fiery carpets under the trees. The unicorns breathed in the fragrance of the crackling, sun-burnished foliage, which like very old silk disintegrated immediately if touched. This intoxicating perfume evoked visions. Maia and Endreol rambled through woods as the leaves fell silently as snow, along amazing, endless avenues of spun gold, realising that what counted was the journeying, not the arriving. The trees whispered the tales of Mother Earth to the two elusive creatures mistaken for light beams.

At last they sensed they were nearing their destination. Something in the sky was familiar, the shape of clouds as they fell

109

like soft cloaks over hillsides. The excited ground sent waves of elation through their weary hooves, making them believe they could dance again.

Soon the pull of the oak trees was unmistakable, like fine wire in the ether. They turned into a field where the kindly Oak Circle stood waiting for them.

The harvest had been gathered and nearby fields ploughed. White birds rose in clusters. It was early evening and after the warmth of the day a mist had risen, gently shrouding everything. Through the mist and what they had first thought was the reflection of the dying Sun, flares were visible, the outline of a huge tent.

Maia and Endreol drew closer. The mist touched their manes and turned into tiny pearls. The gypsy music broke across the fields, tempting everything to listen.

110

The unicorns peeped inside the alluring canvas structure at the exact moment the entire audience held its breath.

High up – a star twinkling with sequins – the wire walker tripped lightly out, exquisitely balanced, fearless, and with total trust….

Dream Softly

A UNICORN DANCED IN THE WOODS

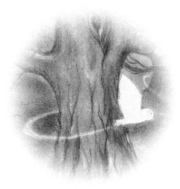

The Elementals

THERE was a great stirring beneath the soil. Sleep of winter was becoming dream of spring when the Mother opened her eyes and breathed out renewal. Deep roots of the oaks throbbed with the hidden energy and the trees appeared to be dancing though standing still. With each new breath of the Mother the birds soared

114

higher, trying to touch the Sun. Their wings were like rainbows as they circled on warm currents that lifted them as carefully as huge, gentle hands. They whistled as sweetly as sacred flutes and the heartbeat of the Mother was a drum summoning all to restored life.

The air was busy with tiny winged creatures, only visible to small children and those psychically attuned to their higher vibration. Elementals, the faerie people, whose task was to help the Mother spin her dreams, used the finest threads and most subtle and radiant colours. Earth Magic was visible everywhere. Spring was as irresistible as romance. She held out her arms promising total fulfilment when she showered blossom which the Wind carried as playfully as birds, whose only reason for being was to celebrate.

In the very early morning when the first light was softly breaking over the fields, tiny beings awoke, stretched and yawned, pulling themselves from under the petals of buttercups and daisies or where they had been sleeping in the vacated homes of snails, or hammocked in cobwebs, wrapped in white feathers and discarded fur. They crept from beneath the roots of the oaks where the fine soil made a comfy mattress. It was difficult to distinguish the texture of their clothes from leaves and flowers. They wore pretty butterfly wing skirts, waistcoats as velvety as the bodies of bees. Their ears were always pointed though their other features and characteristics were diverse. They were whisper smooth or rough as bark. They smelt of damp earth and lilac. They travelled on birds, rode caterpillars, and danced with moths.

As the Sun grew warmer the energy created a frenzy of activity. There was no time to be lost, although in reality it was impossible to lose or measure time. But there was an urgency, a need for each blueprint to be precisely and perfectly manifested. Manifestation is the most creative and inspiring of all the gifts of Nature. To every

116

Elemental a task had been given. Countless activities blended together into millions of miracles.

In spring each sense was heightened. It was impossible to decide which sense was most beautiful. To touch, smell, and see a fragrant flower, or listen to a stream, released a potent chemistry.

Maia and Endreol, nestled in the roots of Ariel, stretched as dawn filtered through the branches, They had been dreaming, down, down into the crystalline energy with snaking roots that held so much mystery in the darkness. In the dreaming they expanded and danced with other unicorns. The early Sun penetrated the leaves creating the finest of patterns as the mild Wind caressed the oak trees.

117

Everything was still half-asleep. They sky was pale pink and the flimsiest mist hovered over the fields which threw up intoxicating newness. Birds flew in slow motion and their cries echoed across the hedgerows shimmering with tiny beings whose auras twinkled like stars. These moments after dawn were the clearest and most illuminating of any day. There was space, calm, and peace. No tension or rush because everything followed the natural process of waiting to be revealed.

Each day was uniquely different. Each month held certain qualities, sometimes the complete opposite. March, dominion of the Wind and the uncatchable hare. Yellow of daffodil, primrose, and dandelion bringing Sun joy. April, the sweetest of all months, carrier of pale and deep pink blossom. May, when leaves are fullest and greenest.

119

Maia and Endreol could see the faeries going about their work as they wandered in the fields nibbling the lush grass. Ariel, Dorc, Swinbourne, and Someil had their own small army of gnomes who were present on every branch, busy with intricate maintenance. Their features were irregular and their eyes leaf green. Strands of silvery hair fell from their hoods, which caused them to look enigmatic and monk-like. Their jackets were as green as their eyes and they wore dark brown waistcoats with acorn buttons. Their boots reached their knees and the tops were folded over, decorated at each side with oak leaves. They smoked pipes filled with a finely ground mixture of acorns and oak apples. As they worked they chanted songs, old as the most ancient woodlands. Songs that had never been written down but contained magical rhythms and nuances the lofty trees responded to, which enabled them to renew themselves endlessly. When the afternoons were hot the gnomes fell asleep in vacant birds' nests, dreaming tree dreams until the lengthening shadows woke them, and they began to toil again.

The white owl, who also shared the oaks' secrets, was woken by the stars and flew in and out of the silhouettes of the giants, with the elusiveness of an angel. The tips of his wings were touched by the waxing Moon. At night activities were of a more esoteric nature. During daylight attention was paid to colour, form, and substance. Nocturnal concerns took on a more spiritual slant. During the deceptively still hours luminosity was created, atmosphere, and the exquisite perfume of flowers – in a huge cauldron that reflected moonbeams and held insect hum. Bird song – from the earliest dawn cries to the piercing notes of the nightingale – was also mixed.

Chirp of cricket and drone of bumble bee came from the dark;

121

screech of the bat moving faster than lightning or hung head down, wings flimsy as black silk; growl of badger, snout dry with earth as he tunnelled under the starlight. The dark gave shelter, protection, and sleep. There was hardly anything to fear in the unlit spaces. Fear was a phantom on a lame horse. Light overcame darkness, always, just as resurrection followed death. Circles and cycles returning to what appeared to be the beginning, but was a new place. The energy at the centre of the Oak Circle was particularly potent. Any creature experiencing this energy felt immediately uplifted and transformed.

As April became May the grass grew more lush, clover thicker. But as the frenzied activity increased the oak trees became calmer, more still. The power of the Earth rose up their trunks, pulsated through branches.

Maia and Endreol played as innocently as children. Hiding and seeking, rolling over and over in the scented grass, sleeping in the warm afternoons, droned into dreams by insects harnessed and ridden by Elementals whose wings and markings were so similar they served as camouflage.

These afternoon dreams were the deepest and softest of all.

Roses and sweet peas were the task of the most talented faerie painters, for the hues and fragrances were divine. During the afternoon dreaming they travelled to the workshops where these miracles were produced: colour combinations that rivalled sunsets and rises; heady perfumes able instantly to pull all those who inhaled them up into a higher dimension.

Wild flowers were tended by faeries who came in on a special ray. They were wilder in spirit than the most playful untamed

123

breeze, adverse to any kind of system, structure, or patterning. They worked where they pleased, scattering seeds and collecting pollen in lonely, uncontaminated places.

They rolled, somersaulted, and flew, hiding in long grass that was half as high as a tree. Their artwork was organic, naive, and impressive for they were able to sweep across the whole of a meadow or the side of a hedgerow with the daintiest flowers and blossom. They loved all that overgrew, tangled, exploded, and twined. Using vines and creepers as circus artists used ropes, they swung through undergrowth faster than sunbeams, were as unpredictable as grasshoppers. They rode on the slippery backs of toads.

Deep in the woods lived the most reclusive sprites. They were hardly distinguishable from tiny shadows. They relished peace, breathing it in with the musky fragrance of dry leaves and the

124

hidden places where the slow-worm twisted, that held the same resonance as ancient chapels and caves. Their clothes were darkest brown and deepest green. It was difficult to see their half-lit faces that like candles were constantly shifting expression. Their shoes had very long, curled up points. Their eyes were impenetrable, and so were their secrets. They spoke in whispers as warm as owls' hoots. Their laughter was able to reach the loneliest heart. When they laughed branches shook with high mirth. They stuck out their round bellies stuffed with hazelnuts and juicy berries.

In the unseen places bird song was created by tiny musicians who patiently experimented to find exactly the right notes for each size, design, and species of bird. The air was full of music, singers and pipers of indecipherable messages breaking into fine frequencies only understood by humans on an unconscious level but which soothed and elated. They absorbed the birds' ecstasy,

125

the chorus formed of so many different notes and sequences that never clashed but blended perfectly in a natural jazz.

The music faeries were hardest of all to see because they were closest to the Element of Air. They were never still, but constantly changed tone, shape and hue, like the music they created.

Light was the most magical thing, whether the dawn light of the rising Sun, fading twilight, or the light of the Moon which fell into fast-moving streams and became jewels, or fingered the mighty oaks so they appeared to be shimmering.

A UNICORN DANCED IN THE WOODS

At the time of the harvest there were delightful celebrations when the Elemental Kingdom came together as one. Each elf, gnome, pixie, faerie, sprite, brought a gift and these were laid out in the Oak Circle. When the parties ended each selected a gift to take away – a frog skin waistcoat, necklace of dew, cloak of butterfly wings, or tiny pumps laced with cobwebs. There were also delicious edibles carried on petals; nectar, jellies and syrups in acorn cups; and crust of honeycomb.

They came countless and overflowing with love and generosity. Their wings moved so fast they were invisible and their weight was not enough to bend a blade of grass. Orchestras of insects and birds were drawn around them. They slid down wheels of golden hay spinning joyously across fields. Banding together they plucked the reddest apples and most succulent blackberries.

128

Under the oaks they feasted until sunset. Then lanterns were lit. The dancing began. Jigs, reels, and rounds went on late into the night. Tiny fiddlers and pipers created the gayest sounds. A sea of faerie folk moved in swarms across the sleeping fields.

Celebrations coincided with the Moon high above the oaks, delicately slipping through the inky sky and each night growing into her fullness. When her magnificent mirror hung low and dazzling over the hedgerows the parties were at their merriest and most abandoned. Silver foxes were drawn from their dens and harvest mice were lost and fat in the corn.

The Moon was so bright she created a different time, neither day or night, but a magical half-time. Trees danced with their shadows and all was fully awake. Faerie fiddlers fiddled into the dawn where the sleepiest stars still twinkled in the pale lemon sky. Then the Elementals dispersed in the mist.

129

Maia and Endreol joined the celebrations. The faeries rode on their backs and whispered in their ears in a language as exquisite as the sound of fluttering leaves and dying bonfires.

Days arrived when the Sun began to withdraw. Crows floated on the North Wind as it pinched the oaks and pulled the hedges out of shape. But all was in its season and by now underground larders were full to overflowing and seeds stored carefully away until they were ready to break open. Earth was heavy and stripped bare. The unicorns awoke covered in frost, and the dry leaves they slept upon were iced with intricate designs.

Winter was the busiest time for the Elementals. It was then that all the spade work was done, sifting, separating, fusing, discarding, furrowing, sowing, and planting. Everything had to be prepared for the moment when new shoots formed, as if by a miracle, when really it was the toil of thousands of tiny beings who chanted, cast spells, and kept warm at night in rabbit holes and the secret chambers of moles.

Ariel, Dorc, Swinbourne, and Someil surveyed the changing landscape as they had done through the centuries, Ageless in age, their heavy branches in a tight cosmic embrace. They were the Wise Ones and the spirits of the oaks tree were among the most beautiful to behold. They wore the palest green robes as filmy as the finest mists that flowed and folded about their fluid form. Their long hair rippled in wispy twigs and their eyes shone with love. Whenever they moved they showered acorns all around them.

The oak trees dreamt of winter, awoke to find birds nesting. Hysteria of gnats was drawn from ponds by sunshine full of hope. Each variety of tree had its own spirits and at dawn or twilight they would come to dance in the Oak Circle, skipping and swirling, merging one with the other, round and round. Ash, birch, beech,

131

cedar, chestnut, hawthorn, maple, walnut, apple, peach, pear, and cherry.

Great spirals of energy charged the atmosphere and drew Spring out of hiding. Her first gift was snowdrops and then she spread primroses through the woods. By February fields of daffodils were waiting to welcome baby rabbits and new lambs. This was the birthing time.

Maia and Endreol awoke earlier, wandered through grove and thicket until sunset. There was a promise of warmth some evenings, although often the warmer the day, the harder the frost that followed. All would be petrified but gradually recover in the sparkling light. The Sun controlled everything, a clock never needing winding or setting for its timing was set by unseen hands.

On the first day of May another spectacular gathering was staged by the Elementals. The Rites of Spring ceremony was held when the sap rose euphorically through the trunks and branches of the oaks. It was time to celebrate the colour rays, from the brightest red to the palest violet.

All morning the faeries were busy gathering blossom, flowers, vines, and leaves. At noon they rested, hidden in the long grass that towered above them in a forest. All afternoon the unicorns stood patiently while they were groomed and decorated for the occasion. Their long manes were plaited with daisy chains, and wreaths of wild flowers crowned their heads. They drowned amidst petals, and finely woven creeper was twisted playfully around their legs.

At last the faeries stood back enraptured by their work. A hush fell over the Oak Circle, as if something very special and extraordinary was about to happen. Anticipation, elation, and desire were audible as a joyful radiance was drawn into the sacred space.

133

A faerie cheer greeted the Elemental King and Queen and much curtsying, bowing, and saluting. The bravest dared touch their robes or blew thistledown kisses. They were attended by train-bearers, honeysuckle faeries with the sweetest of smiles, and an army of pixies who found it extremely difficult to act sedately. When they reached the centre of the Oak Circle the King and Queen flew up on to the unicorns' backs. It was hardly possible to distinguish magical beast or faerie from garlands of flowers.

Maia carried the Queen whose grace and beauty mesmerized all. Endreol bore the King, most noble and powerful of beings, Holder and Knower of every spell and secret. His eyes were deep-seeing and his smile like mead.

The excited train-bearers followed Maia and Endreol as they proudly and elegantly paraded. Then, festooned with flowers, the ecstatic unicorns reared up on their hind legs and danced.

134

Thus was celebrated the Rites of Spring......

Dream Forever

A UNICORN DANCED IN THE WOODS

The Watchers

A BOVE the Oak Circle clouds formed and evaporated, purified, puffed, twisted, ballooned, swirled, danced. Calm or angry they were finest lace or an impenetrable blanket hiding the sky. Sometimes when Maia looked up through the branches she could see archangels spanning the ether. Their huge wings rippled

138

like foam as they gazed down benignly over the tree tops. They came from the Higher Dimensions that surrounded the Earth plain in invisible layers.

Each dimension was finer and more beautiful than the one before. The angels came from the holiest place where all Light Beings dwelt and the Higher Selves of men. They protected and guarded Earth's children. Some believed the Higher Selves were angels too, and a fragment of their being had entered into bodies to experience the heaviest level of existence and transform it.

The angels came very close to the unicorn. They were drawn to her purity, and the powerful energy in the Oak Circle made it possible for them to manifest. At Christmas the angels came closer. Their eyes brimmed with candlelight and the sparkle from Christmas trees. Their vibration was crystal clear. Their wings were full of snowflakes, each one unique. They wore the flimsiest

139

of garments as light as rising mist; materialised in silence, exceedingly poignant because of the contrast with all that appeared so solid and heavy.

Angels of snow and mist danced in the Oak Circle and the trees sang carols. The damp bark was darker in winter and acted as an overcoat when all leaves had fallen and acorns were stored, scattered, or eaten. When the angels came the trees felt less exposed and vulnerable, sensed the turn of the year was near and the new cycle of joy was almost ready to begin. Winter was the loveliest season if truly accepted. The oaks etched against the magenta sunsets had experienced his gift many hundreds of times. Winter stripped down to the roots, bared all, tested for strength.

How cold was coldest? How hard could the East Wind blow? How dark and scary were the long nights that overshadowed afternoon?

140

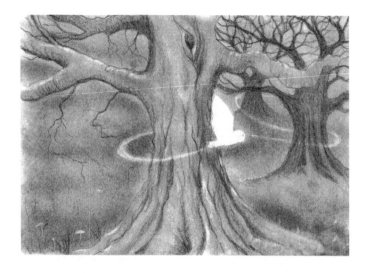

Some mornings the oaks awoke dressed in icicles and patterned with frost. Crows' throats were raw and nothing thawed until noon when the Sun was just strong enough to make a difference. The angels started to appear in December. Days were shorter and the Sun uncertain.

The Yule festival hearkened back to the most archaic times. Time of Druid mysticism and wisdom when trees and men were as

141

one. All these memories, this magic flowed as the robes had flowed over the icy soil where worms, ants, centipedes, and snakes were dormant. The feet of the Druids were bare as they walked in the woodland. They could feel energy bubbling up though it was the winter sleep. Their lanterns cast dancing shadows on the trunks of the oaks.

The Oak Circle was able to hold energy that is timeless. The ground and the stones were as old as time itself. Here had walked the Ancestors whose spirits were now in other dimensions, whose blood had been passed down through the generations. The oak and the stag had long held communion. But the unicorn more elusive, and except on rare occasions visible only in dreams, did not carry the fear of the stag, or that of any other wildlife or species.

The Circle held all that is intangible and yet known. There were many oaks trees of various ages, size, and gender. Some stood

142

close together, others further or far apart. Maia and Endreol spent time with different trees, learning their history and listening to their wisdom, acknowledging them.

In the autumn, before the angels came, the oaks basked in and were drenched by the mellow sunshine. They were able to open the thoughts and hearts of men as if they carried keys. They did this without trying, simple by being there. All those who had not been tuned in but then acknowledged their noble presence, like the unicorns, became free. The unicorns knew the name and disposition of each oak.

The Circle was wide and took a considerable time to work right round. In the West the energy was dense and remote, brambles and hawthorn grew up round the trunks, and holly. There was a hidden away feeling that was both exciting and mysterious. Flash of rabbit tail and the flank of a startled deer dissolving into the undergrowth.

143

But the unicorns moved with such grace that the fight or flight reaction was not triggered.

Although the white owl ruled all this territory there were hovering hawks, mere specks in the sky until they telescoped down to take helpless field mice in their claws. There was always pain present, for pain was a necessary part of the Creation, the perfect opposite of pleasure.

The trees in the West held the Sun in their branches in the evenings.

Each tree had a soul. Canton was a great grandfather. He was knobbly and extremely rough. He was the tallest. He had fought many times with the Wind and his sturdy limbs were strewn around his base. His sweet-smelling body had been used to make fires and his spirit had burnt brightly in the flames. Ezekiel his son, stood next to him and he was the strongest oak in the Circle. His trunk

144

was exceedingly wide and although partly covered with ivy, nothing could ever steal his strength or overwhelm him.

The great grandmother standing to his right was awesome. She had many faces and expressions. She was hard to know, held her story with the same care that she held small nests and fledglings. Hilda was a mother in every sense of the word, great and grand, commanding respect, influencing all that touched her or drew near.

To gradually walk the Circle, resting and communicating with each oak, was to begin to know the secret of its power. Each oak connected with and was programmed by the Great Crystal Skull. The Skull knew when a twig broke off or an acorn fell. The trees responded to and experienced each shift in light.

Dawn brought total rebirth and nightfall a death that became transformation in the starshine.

145

At night the Circle gave the appearance of sleep but the night energy coaxed out foxes, badgers, weasels, and all those creatures which preferred to hide and be hidden. Darkness could be experienced as a threat or protection.

The oaks dreamed the night dream, detached from each other but powerful in being so many together and because the Circle was unbroken. Claws and teeth of moonlight prowlers, cats wandered far away from home, swooping bats, flying dragon. Tunnelling rabbits, safe in deep, warm burrows.

All was beautiful and had its reason. The shades of night were only the subconscious spilling out as sleep allowed the freedom to rise up unfettered like the owl. When the Sun rose, touching the easterly arc of the Circle, all that was predatory and disturbing disappeared and that which slept awoke.

The oaks in the East of the Circle were more elusive of spirit.

146

They waved from a distance, were airy and heavily populated by birds and flying insects. Many feathers were scattered around their trunks. They were the youngest trees. They awoke enervated and pulled solar energy from the horizon up through the atmosphere so that everything became lucid. Energy was fast-moving at this point of the Circle, and Maia and Endreol felt the exhilaration penetrating their hooves.

The trees grouped together and were named as groups. There were the Wise Ones, the Seers.

In the South of the Oak Circle the trees were extremely strong and individual. They were neither young nor ancient but had a fullness and maturity that was magnetic, uplifting, and calming. They were the Watchers and the Waiters. Their truly inspirational thoughts went out through the ether for many miles. They were able to reach the highest and lowest realms, to ground, lift, expand

147

and heal. They were the grandmothers and grandfathers of tomorrow.

And in the centre of the Circle, in line, were Ariel, Dorc, Swinbourne, and Someil, the wisest and most revered of all trees. Here lived the white owl, wisest of all birds. The Ancestors came back through the many dimensional doorways as guides. No one on the Earth plain walked alone. In such power points as this circle, it was easier to link with them.

Many days and many seasons had passed since Maia and Endreol had been married in the wonderful Oak Circle wedding Occasionally there had been separations, times when either or both needed to be alone on their journey. These spaces and separations deepened their understanding. When they reunited progressed, the coming together was electrifying. They cantered joyfully and their horns shimmered.

Now it was autumn again. Leaves were falling in showers which carpeted the woods. The unicorns' hooves sank into the aromatic, rustling drifts and they rolled on their backs allowing the horse spirit freedom. The brambles were heavy with blackberries, and shiny red berries shouted to be noticed. There was an entwining of wild flowers and creeper. Butterflies soared high as birds.

There was peace among the trees which held out their branches to be hugged by the Sun that was unafraid of dying. But something

150

was stirring here. The oak trees sensed it. There was anticipation. Something unspoken, unwritten, but known, was made conscious by a sixth sense.

The stars glittered in the autumn fall, flashing and shooting, clusters of awe-inspiring brilliance. This was the night sky where the Ancestors had found guidance. They had understood the mathematics and heeded the messages. The trines, squares and oppositions of the planets had masterminded evolution. How tantalising was the mystery with no beginning and no end, like a circle twisting into infinity.

The Wise Ones had always been in the stars, somewhere.

On Christmas Eve a new formation appeared in the galaxies above the Oak Circle. It was in the shape of a unicorn standing high and proud on her hind legs. Her horn was a column of stars flickering and twinkling.

151

The air was clear, sharp and extremely cold, dizzy with expectation as the white owl took his evening flight. He flew around each tree and then high over the Oak Circle beneath the Cosmic Unicorn. When he returned to his home in the great oak Ariel he looked down and saw Maia and Endreol curled up sleeping. Between the roots of the tree that were like huge toes, almost hidden in leaves, was the tiniest unicorn imaginable.

On Christmas morning there were a few flurries of snow and the ground was unyielding. The sky was grey at first but when the Sun appeared lightened, and gradually became vibrant blue. Then it was possible to see that the flurries were the wings of angels.

Snow began to settle. Small boot prints appeared in tracks that led into the woods. Little gnarled men with skin as rough and tough as bark carried gifts for the newborn creature - feathers, leaves, and fur. The smoke from their pipes smelt like incense and

152

their eyes were full of fire.

The tiny unicorn was named Crystal and she carried the clearest and purest energy.

As the day passed the snow became deeper and sound was muffled. Gradually the Oak Circle filled with flying beings as fragile as snowflakes, each one carrying a light. And all creatures not in hibernation came too. Those who slept came in their dreams. The essence of the wildlife resonated in the Circle – softness of rabbit, swiftness of deer, cunning of fox, playfulness of squirrel, slowness of badger, speed and skill of spider - her web laced with minute crystals. This essence filled the ether like a Christmas carol.

When the snow stopped falling the Sun came out again, low in the sky above the West of the Oak Circle – and then fell slowly down behind the crowns of the mighty trees in a fantastic mix of colours intermingled with gold, rose, violet, and purple. The snow

153

reflected the sky – and all the trees and the creatures in them, above them and beneath them, soaked up this vibrancy. The clouds formed into archangels, dragons, and unicorns floating over the oaks in a spectacular Christmas carnival.

The white owl flew out across the Circle joining the pageant.

As the Sun set, Maia, Endreol, and Crystal left their shelter beneath Ariel and made their way nimbly across the snow. When they reached the centre of the Oak Circle they rose up on their hind legs and danced a dance of ecstasy......

Dream Awake

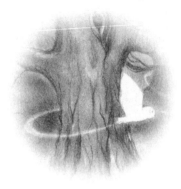

Crystal

FOR many days the tiny unicorn stayed safely beside Maia and Endreol. She moved about within their shadows, intensely happy and excited. Everything she beheld filled her with wonder – a buzzing bee, a leaf being blown by the Wind, the guardian oaks that towered above her and seemed to touch the fast-

157

moving sky. She had no past and no future, only NOW. Now was simply a choice of focus.

The hues of Earth Mother were so varied and so beautiful. Green dominated the Oak Circle, the colour of leaves and grass. There were so many greens. Green was connected to the heart and being in the trees, away from human confusion, heightened the feelings and allowed love to be felt and expressed more easily.

But Crystal knew nothing of cities or even villages. She knew nothing of humans, although she had once heard gun shots in the woods and had instinctively fled. Although the ugly sound reached her she was in no danger for she was invisible to all but a few. To see a unicorn required the inner sense of small children.

Each moment offered new sensations, delicious experiences. Everything kept magically changing. She slept in a nest of spring flowers, breathing in the sweetest perfume. And when she awoke

158

early, the Sun would be peeping over the dancing stalks. Crystal stretched in the dappled light, awaking from sleeping dreams into waking dreams. Both sort depended on the imagination of the dreamer.

Maia and Endreol did not attempt to teach her anything. She held the secret knowledge within. But they gave her confidence to expand, to reach out, merely by their commanding and reassuring presence.

It was Time of the Unicorn. Each tree, each being in the Oak Circle sensed the shift and was filled with anticipation and longing. The white owl watched and waited. He felt the heartbeat of the oaks as he perched on their branches. He had the overview, rising high on his delicately balanced wings, till even the oaks shrunk into miniature and were smaller than the span of his feathers.

159

He loved night when he absorbed the beams of the Moon and listened to the silent stars.

Crystal heard his mysterious Om floating through the darkness as she snuggled up in her perfumed nest. Each time she slept she grew a little. Once she was big enough to leave the Oak Circle she wandered far into the woods, through the shadows and clearings. Everything enthralled her. She was mesmerized by dragonflies with glittering wings, skimming the surface of shining ponds. Water mirrored, hypnotised everything. And she gazed at the upside down world that appeared perfectly when all was perfectly still.

"*Crystal…. CRY-STAL.*" She intuited Maia and Endreol urging her home, through the ether telepathically. So she returned to the Oak Circle at twilight.

Crystal's mission was to take what Maia and Endreol had brought to the Earth plain to a new level, as each generation has the potential to do. But how she was to achieve this was still hidden from her. And she was hardly conscious anyway of having a mission. She would pass through this initiation at some stage. All she needed was to be fully alert.

Then the lucid dream came to her as she lay sleeping under the oaks. A splendid unicorn appeared. He showed her esoteric places, realms few had visited. He guided her to the chamber of the Crystal Skull which Maia had long ago ventured into so bravely. "You are the lightest, brightest creature that has ever existed on

Earth," the unicorn told her. "You will enter the visions and dreams of the sleepwalkers and gently awaken them."

But how to enter others' dreams? How was that possible? The master unicorn whose name was Defieus, paced the Oak Circle with the little unicorn who was as eager as early morning.

"You have two teachers," he explained, "the Moon and the white owl. Observe them well and pay heed to what they show you. The ancient oaks will give you strength. Learn your lessons well, dear one."

And then Crystal *AWOKE*.

A UNICORN DANCED IN THE WOODS

Writer and painter Christine Day is inspired by Nature and the esoteric. The first journalist on the London pop scene to interview the Who and the Moody Blues, she also met Bowie and Hendrix when they emerged on the scene. Her features on astrology, the aura, healing, and alternative therapies helped bring into the mainstream what were considered taboo subjects. She has profiled celebrities for Hello magazine, campaigned to save threatened buildings, endangered wildlife, and displaced people. She is a qualified spiritual psychotherapist. Her books include Jappy A Spiritual Cat, A Retro Collection of 70's and 80's Short Stories, and The Name On The Mirror.

christinedaywriter.weebly.com/www.christineday.co.uk

Artist John Wakefield is known for his beautiful paintings and delightful illustrations. He works intuitively with Nature, the seasons, and the magical elements that hold everything together. He lives in West Sussex where he finds inspiration walking in the woodlands and fields. ***www.jwakefield.co.uk***